First published in Spanish as *Camino a casa* by
Jairo Buitrago and Rafael Yockteng
Copyright © 2008 by Fondo de Cultura Económica
Carretera Picacho Ajusco 227, C.P. 14378, México, D.F.
English translation copyright © 2017 by Elisa Amado
First published in English in Canada and the USA in 2017
by Groundwood Books
Second printing 2017

Groundwood Books / House of Anansi Press
groundwoodbooks.com

With the participation of the Government of Canada | Canadä
Avec la participation du gouvernement du Canada

Library and Archives Canada Cataloguing in Publication
Buitrago, Jairo
[Camino a casa. English]
Walk with me / written by Jairo Buitrago ; illustrated by
Rafael Yockteng; translated by Elisa Amado.
Translation of: Camino a casa.
Issued in print and electronic formats.
ISBN 978-1-55498-857-0 (bound). —
ISBN 978-1-55498-858-7 (pdf)
 I. Yockteng, Rafael, illustrator II. Amado, Elisa, translator
III. Title. IV. Title: Camino a casa. English.
PZ7.B8857Wa 2017   j863'.7   C2015-904608-4
C2015-904609-2

The illustrations were sketched in pencil, scanned and then
redrawn and colored digitally.
Design adapted by Michael Solomon from an original
design by Gabriela Martínez Nava
Printed and bound in Malaysia

To my Dama Roja — RY

Jairo Buitrago

Translated by Elisa Amado

PICTURES BY
Rafael Yockteng

WALK WITH ME

GROUNDWOOD BOOKS HOUSE OF ANANSI PRESS TORONTO BERKELEY

Keep me company on the way home,

then I can have someone to
talk to so I don't fall asleep

on the long walk out of the city.

Let's go as fast as we can,

then wait for me.

Let's go together into
the neighborhood,

and to the store that won't give
us credit anymore.

Eat with us

and, if you like, you can wait till
Mama gets home from the factory.

If you'd rather, you could go up into the hills again.

But then come back when I call.

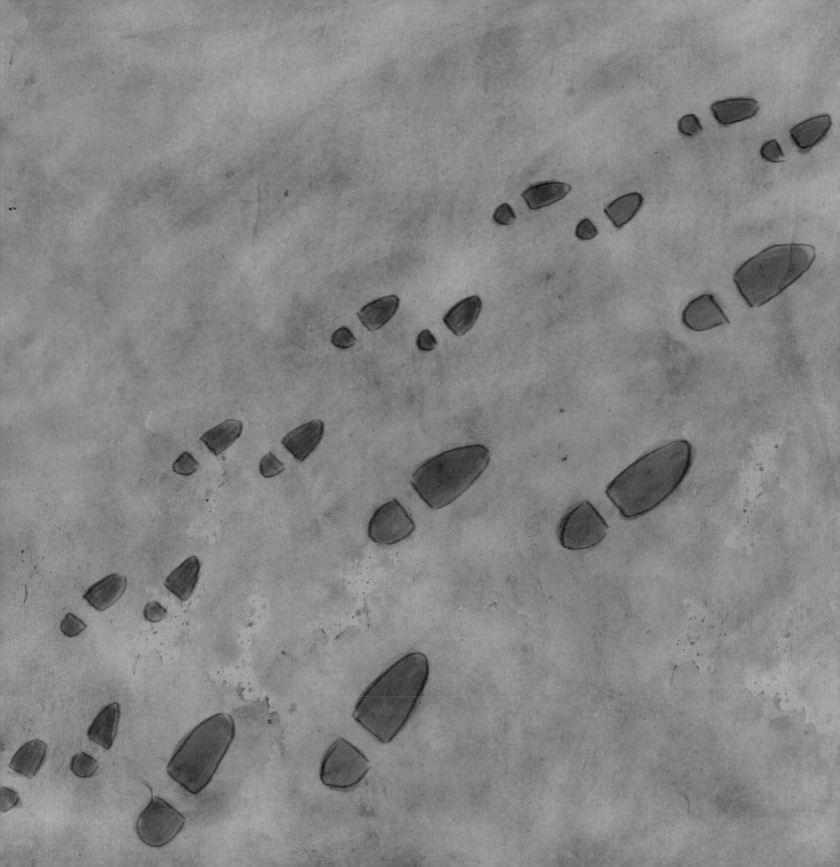